Arthur and the Poetry Contest

A Marc Brown ARTHUR Chapter Book

Arthur and the Poetry Contest

Text by Stephen Krensky

Based on a teleplay by Joe Fallon

Little, Brown and Company

Boston   New York   London

J
FICTION
B RO

For the Richard O'Connor family

Text has been reviewed and assigned a reading level by Laurel S. Ernst, M.A., Teachers College, Columbia University, New York, New York; reading specialist, Chappaqua, New York

The following poems appear in this book:

"The Walrus and the Carpenter" (page 15) by Lewis Carroll, from *Through the Looking-Glass* (1872); "Locksley Hall" (page 15) by Alfred, Lord Tennyson (1842); "The Sleeper" (page 17) by Edgar Allan Poe (1831); "Paul Revere's Ride" (page 18) by Henry Wadsworth Longfellow, from *Tales of a Wayside Inn* (1863); "My Sister Is a Sissy," (pages 2–3) and "Today Is Very Boring" (pages 38–40) from *The New Kid on the Block* by Jack Prelutsky, text copyright © 1984 by Jack Prelutsky, reprinted by permission of Greenwillow Books, a division of William Morrow & Company Inc.

Library of Congress Cataloging-in-Publication Data

Krensky, Stephen.
Arthur and the poetry contest / text by Stephen Krensky. — 1st ed.
    p.   cm. — (A Marc Brown Arthur chapter book ; 18)
"Based on a teleplay by Joe Fallon."
    Summary: Fern dares Arthur and his friends to enter the poetry writing contest at the local library, but writing poems turns out to be harder than they thought.
    ISBN 0-316-12062-6 (hc) — ISBN 0-316-12295-5 (pb)
    [1. Poetry Fiction. 2. Contests Fiction. 3. Aardvark Fiction.
4. Animals Fiction.] I. Title. II. Series: Brown, Marc Tolon. Marc
Brown Arthur chapter book; 18.
PZ7.K883 Ap 1999
[Fic] — dc21   99-35270

10 9 8 7 6 5 4 3 2 1

WOR (hc)
COM-MO (pb)

Printed in the United States of America

Chapter 1

• • • • • • • • • • •

Mr. Ratburn stood at the front of the class. He was holding a list of names. At least, it was supposed to be a list. However, there was only one name on it, which made it barely a list at all.

"There are only two days left until the library poetry contest," he told the class. "This is supposed to be the list of participants. But so far, only one student—Fern—has signed up."

Everyone turned to look at Fern. She stared at the floor.

"Fern never said she wrote poetry," Francine whispered.

1

"Fern never says anything," Muffy reminded her.

"Writing poetry is worse than eating snails," said Binky. "If I wrote it, I wouldn't admit it, either."

Mr. Ratburn cleared his throat. "The judge for this contest is the famous poet Jack Prelutsky. And it's still not too late to enter."

"I'm a poet and I don't even know it," said Buster.

"You've got a rhyme every time," Muffy added.

Arthur raised his hand. "I know a poem he wrote. It's called 'My Sister Is a Sissy.' "

"Can you recite it for us?" asked Mr. Ratburn.

Arthur wasn't sure. "I'll try," he said.

"My sister is a sissy,
she's afraid of dogs and cats,
a toad can give her tantrums,

and she's terrified of rats,
she screams at things with stingers,
things that buzz, and things that crawl,
just the shadow of a spider
sends my sister up the wall.

"A lizard makes her shiver,
and a turtle makes her squirm,
she positively cringes
at the prospect of a worm,
she's afraid of things with feathers,
she's afraid of things with fur,
she's scared of almost everything —
how come I'm scared of her?

"That's all," said Arthur, pleased he could remember it.

"If D.W. were my sister," Francine whispered to Muffy, "I'd be afraid of her, too."

"An excellent poem," Mr. Ratburn noted. "And speaking as someone who has a sister, I can agree with the sentiment."

He sighed. "Now, I know a lot of you may not have thought much about poetry before, but it is truly one of the most powerful — and fun — literary forms. It is also one of the oldest. The Trojan War, for example, was described in a long poem by the Greek poet Homer in around 900 B.C. The poem is called 'The Iliad.'"

Binky frowned. "Isn't that the story where some soldiers hid inside a horse?"

"Exactly," said Mr. Ratburn.

"The horse was the source of the force — of course!" commented the Brain.

Everyone laughed.

"You're all very talented," Mr. Ratburn continued, "which is why I'm encouraging you to enter the contest. As a special treat, Mr. Prelutsky will be speaking at the Elwood City Library after school on Thursday."

Francine nudged Arthur. "Listen, I'm a poet. Moon, June, spoon, tune — a loon."

"Will you be done soon?" Arthur asked.

"Before noon," Francine replied sweetly.

Arthur was glad to hear it.

Chapter 2

• • • • • • • • • • • •

It was just after twelve when the class ate lunch in the cafeteria. Fern sat alone, working on her poem while she ate.

Binky and Rattles started talking as they approached her table.

"Just thinking about poetry makes me sleepy," said Binky. He let out a big yawn. Then he closed his eyes and began to snore.

"Hey, Binky!" said Rattles. "Wake up!"

Binky fell back limply, but Rattles reached out to catch him.

"Come on, Binky," said Rattles. "I've got a question for you."

Binky opened one eye. "What?"

"What's twice as boring as a poem?"

Binky frowned. "I give up."

"Two poems!"

A lot of the kids nearby laughed.

But not Fern. She gathered her things and stood up. "You only make fun," she told Binky, "because you couldn't write a poem if your life depended on it."

Then she walked out.

All the kids gasped.

Francine was impressed. "That's the most Fern has said all year."

"And it was well put," the Brain noted.

Binky didn't like the way everyone was giggling at him. He ran to catch up with Fern. The other kids followed him out.

Fern and Binky faced each other in the hall.

"What do you want now?" Fern asked.

Binky put his hands on his hips. "Maybe I couldn't write a poem *fast*," he told her.

"But neither could they," he added, pointing to the other kids.

"Wait a minute!" said Francine. "I could if I *wanted* to."

"Me, too," said Arthur. "No problem."

Binky stared at them. "Hah! I could write a better poem than you with my brain tied behind my back."

"Really?" said Arthur, snickering. "I'd like to see that."

"Oh, you would, would you?"

"Yeah! That's what I said!"

Fern stepped between them.

"Hold on," she said. "I'll bet *none* of you can write a decent poem."

"I can so!" Francine insisted.

"Yeah, me, too," said Buster.

"I think *I* can!" Sue Ellen chimed in.

Arthur folded his arms. "Maybe Binky can't, but I can."

"I can do anything Arthur can," Binky declared.

"I can write a poem like *that*," Arthur insisted, trying to snap his fingers.

"Fern, I cannot believe you would question my poetic capability," said the Brain.

"Hold me back!" Binky exclaimed. "Somebody hold me back, or I'll write a poem right now!"

"QUIET!" Fern shouted.

They all closed their mouths at once. It was not that Fern was such a commanding figure. They had just never heard her yell before.

"Now," Fern continued more calmly, "we'll see who can do what. You can each write a poem and enter it in the poetry contest. Anyone who doesn't finish in time has to join the Poetry Club for a whole year. Is it a bet — or are you a bunch of chickens?"

"No problem," said Binky.

"Prepare to be humiliated," the Brain told her.

"I'm ready," said Francine.

"You're going to lose a bet," said Muffy.
Arthur and Buster nodded.

Fern smiled. "Good."

"How do you write a poem?" Arthur whispered to Buster.

Buster shrugged. "I thought you knew."

Arthur shook his head. He had no idea. But how hard could it be?

Chapter 3

· · · · · · · · · · ·

Arthur and Buster entered the library together.

"I don't want to go to Poetry Club for a whole year!" said Arthur.

Buster shuddered. "It would be a fate worse than death. But don't worry. It'll be a cinch to get out of this. We'll just find a good poem and, um, write one like it."

They charged up to the front desk.

"Which way to the good poems?" asked Arthur.

Ms. Turner looked up from her desk.

"The good poems?"

"We're short on time," Buster explained.

"So we don't want to read bad ones. We want to skip right to the good stuff."

"I see," said Ms. Turner. "Do you have any other criteria or guidelines?"

Buster thought for a moment. "Well, we need to be able to understand them."

"Poems we can't understand will not help," Arthur agreed.

"All right," said Ms. Turner. "Do you want old poems or more recent ones?"

"Old," Buster blurted.

"What difference does that make?" Arthur whispered to him.

"If we're going to borrow from poems," said Buster, "it will be better if the poets are dead. That way, they can't get mad at us."

Arthur turned back to the librarian. "Definitely old," he said. "Old, old, old."

With Ms. Turner's help, they quickly gathered armfuls of books and piled them on a table.

Buster flipped one open. "What do you think of this?

"'The time has come,' the Walrus said,
'To talk of many things:
Of shoes—and ships—and sealing wax—
Of cabbages—and kings—
And why the sea is boiling hot—
And whether pigs have wings.'"

Buster stared at the page. "This is goofy. I don't think I can write like this."

Arthur agreed. "Let's find one that makes more sense."

Buster flipped through another book and read:

"Something better than his dog,
a little dearer than his horse."

Buster frowned. "What does *that* mean?"

"Maybe it's a riddle," said Arthur. "What's better than his dog, a little deer, and then his horse?"

"I know, I know!" cried Buster. "A gerbil that can do your homework."

"I've never heard of a gerbil like that."

"Me, neither," Buster admitted. "But wouldn't it be neat?"

Arthur closed the book. "I think we should just skip this guy."

Buster picked up a book entitled *Tales and Poems of Edgar Allan Poe.*

"Whoa! Listen to these titles! 'The Haunted Palace' and 'The Conqueror Worm.' " He started reading aloud.

"It was the dead who groaned within."

Arthur's eyes opened wide. "Wow! Still a little strange, though. Here's one that sounds more familiar.

*"Listen, my children, and you shall hear
Of the midnight ride of Paul Revere."*

"That has a good beat," said Arthur.

"Kind of like a horse galloping," Buster noted. "Hey! Paul Revere was riding a horse. Do you think the poet did that on purpose?"

"He might have. Poets are tricky like that."

"Not me," said Buster. "When I write my poem, everything will be very clear."

"You mean, you're ready?"

"Yup," said Buster. "Aren't you?"

"I guess," said Arthur, who didn't want to fall behind. "My poem is right up here," he added, pointing to his head.

But just *where* up there, even he didn't know.

Chapter 4

• • • • • • • • • • •

At lunch the next day, everyone was discussing the poetry contest.

"My poem is turning out to be long," said Sue Ellen. "I'm only about halfway done."

Binky laughed. "Mine is short. Short and sweet."

"More like short because short means less work, right?" said Sue Ellen.

Binky nodded. "That's what makes it sweet," he explained.

Buster finished slurping his milk through a straw and turned to Arthur.

"How long did you work on your poem last night?"

Arthur wasn't sure. "Um, I was pretty busy. I had to clean my room and line up the books on my shelves. There were pencils to sharpen, and I emptied my wastebasket—twice. Then I took Pal for a walk. Oh, and D.W. needed help with her homework...."

"D.W. has homework?" said Buster. "Yikes! Times sure have changed since I was in preschool."

"Well, it wasn't homework exactly," Arthur admitted. "She was coloring in a picture."

"Oooooh!" said Binky. "That sounds tricky. How were you helping?"

"I made sure she stayed inside the lines."

Binky let out a deep breath. "That's a *big* job."

"Yeah, yeah," said Buster. "So, Arthur, what's your poem about?"

"About?"

"You know, the subject, the main idea."

"Um, it's kind of hard to say."

"Uh-oh," said Buster. "I hope it's not like some of those poems we looked at yesterday. You know, the poems that are supposed to mean something, but you can never figure out what that something is. And even if you could, you wouldn't be able to understand it because the words are too big."

"Don't worry," said Arthur. "When the poem is clear to me, it will be clear to you, too."

Buster was relieved.

"The Brain," Fern announced, "has finished his poem."

Arthur was shocked. "Already? What did you do, push a button?"

The Brain nodded. "Something like that.

Can I read it to you? Any helpful comments are welcome."

He pulled out a piece of paper and began to read.

"I, the Brain, will explain what makes rain.
Water droplets are what clouds contain,
They reach saturation,
Become precipitation,
Hit the ground,
And roll right down the drain."

"Wow!" said Buster. "It rhymes *and* it's educational."

"I'm done, too!" said Muffy. She pulled out her own paper.

"My favorite thing to do is shop,
For shoes, shirts, coats, rings,
(You can never have enough jewelry)
And games, until I drop.
I love to shop."

"That's not a poem," said Buster. "It's a list."

"A list can be a poem," replied Muffy. "Besides, *shop* rhymes with *drop*."

Arthur looked worried. Even a shopping poem would have looked good to him—if he had managed to write one. But Arthur had nothing written yet. Nothing at all.

Chapter 5

· · · · · · · · · · · ·

Arthur sat in his room that night working on his poem. He wrote,

Listen my children as I tell you

That was good, of course, at least for a start. Unfortunately, it didn't go very far. Who should be the main characters?

Listen my children as I tell you
About a duck and a chicken

Well, that was okay. A duck and a chicken could be friends or just traveling together. But where were they going? And how was he going to make it rhyme?

Listen my children as I tell you
About a duck and a chicken
On a bus to Oklahomu

Arthur slumped forward at his desk. *Oklahomu?* This was not going at all the way he had hoped.

His door opened.

"Arthur, did you hear the news?"

It was D.W.

Arthur raised his head. "Don't you ever knock?"

"No. Why bother?"

Arthur shook his head. "Little sisters should always knock. It should be a law. Whatever you want, D.W., now is a bad time. Can't you see I'm trying to work?"

"You didn't look like you were working. You looked like you were sleeping."

"Not now, D.W...."

"Anyway, I came in to tell you about this news flash on the TV."

"Didn't you hear me, D.W.? I HAVE TO WORK!"

"You know, Arthur, getting excited like this will not help you think better."

Arthur put down his pencil. "You're not going to leave until you tell me, are you?"

She smiled at him. "How did you guess? So, there's this gorilla named Joey. He was taken out of the jungle only last week. Now he's escaped from his cage at the zoo."

Arthur was interested in spite of himself. "Where is he now?"

"He climbed up a building. Like King Kong. And now there are helicopters and everything all around him."

"He must be scared," said Arthur. "Maybe he just wants to get home to the jungle."

D.W. shrugged. "I hope he shows up here. I could use a new friend. And he'd be great for show-and-tell."

Arthur sighed. He didn't want to meet Joey unless the gorilla had some good poems to unload.

"You don't seem very happy, Arthur. Are you still doing that dumb poem? Hey, I know a great one for you!

"Roses are red,
Violets are blue,
My nose smells
And your feet do, too."

D.W. rolled on the floor, laughing. Arthur just walked out.

"Doesn't that crack you up, Arthur?" She looked around. "Arthur?"

Arthur had gone into his parents' bedroom to use the phone. He hoped Buster could help him.

"Hello? Buster's the name. Poetry's my game."

"Hi, Buster, it's me, Arthur. I'm glad at least one of us is making progress. When you're done with your poem, can you help me?"

"Sure, Arthur."

"So where are you?"

"About halfway."

"Halfway through the poem?"

"No. Halfway through the first line."

"Oh." Arthur sighed. "Well, then I guess you'll be pretty busy for a while."

"Who knows, Arthur? Lightning might strike at any second!"

"Well, if it does, send some my way."

Then he hung up.

Chapter 6

• • • • • • • • • • • •

The next morning, Arthur gulped down his breakfast.

"Why the big rush?" asked his mother. "Cereal doesn't get soggy *that* fast."

"I'm meeting with Fern before school," Arthur explained.

Mr. Read picked up the newspaper. "Look at this headline. 'TOWN GOES APE.' This gorilla has everybody talking."

"I was hoping he'd stop by our house," said D.W.

Her father smiled. "He'd probably enjoy my banana bread. It says here, they found his trail leading into the woods."

31

"The poor thing," said Mrs. Read. "I'm sure he misses the jungle and all his friends."

"Speaking of friends, I have to go," said Arthur, rushing out the door.

When Arthur got to school, he found Buster and Fern talking on the playground. Fern was making a face.

"How does it start again?" she asked.

Buster cleared his throat.

"Once upon a midnight cloudy,
A big old bat said, 'Howdy, Howdy'!"

Fern waited. Buster waited, too.

"Well?" she asked finally.

"That's as far as I got," Buster admitted.

Fern looked disappointed. "I suppose it's a start."

"*Cloudy* and *howdy* rhyme," Buster pointed out.

"I noticed. But a poem doesn't have to rhyme, and rhyming by itself doesn't make a poem work."

Buster frowned. "I was afraid you'd say that."

Fern looked at Arthur. "What about yours?" she asked.

Arthur didn't even want to read his poem aloud. He just handed it to her.

Fern read it quickly. *"Oklahomu?* Boy, Arthur, I know you can do better than that. Besides, this poem seems a little familiar. Instead of copying other people, you need to be original. Use your imagination."

"I don't have any ideas," said Buster.

"You have to be excited when you write a poem," Fern told him. "If you're not excited writing it, nobody will be excited reading it. But don't feel boxed in. A poem can be about anything — something in your life, something you heard about. There's no limit."

"You really believe people would want to hear what I think about?" Buster asked.

Fern shrugged. "There's only one way to find out."

Later, at recess, while the other kids were playing, Arthur and Buster worked on their poems. Arthur was lying on the ground, and Buster sat perched on a tree branch above him.

Arthur was thinking about what Fern had said. It made sense to use his imagination. The problem was, his imagination seemed to have suddenly gone on vacation. And he had no idea when it was coming back.

Arthur looked up. Buster didn't seem to be having this problem. He was humming to himself as he wrote down one word after another.

"I'm done!" Buster shouted suddenly. "I'm...Whoa! Look out!"

He fell off the branch and landed near Arthur.

"Oof!"

Buster looked down at Arthur. "I'm done!" he said again. "Isn't that great?"

"Great," Arthur repeated. "Now can you get up?"

Buster got to his feet. "I hope I didn't interrupt your thoughts."

Arthur sighed. "No such luck," he said.

Chapter 7

Inside the library that afternoon, Ms. Turner was introducing the guest speaker, Jack Prelutsky. The kids in the audience were gathered around him.

"We're very pleased to have Mr. Prelutsky here with us today," said Ms. Turner. "I won't embarrass him by listing all his awards and honors, but let's just say he's one of our favorites. Please give him a warm Elwood City welcome."

The kids clapped loudly.

"Thank you," said Mr. Prelutsky. "I'm sure that some of you, when trying to write a poem, think you have to start

with something dramatic or important.
Certainly, there's nothing wrong with that.
But some of the best poems seem to pop
up out of everyday things. For example,

"Today is very boring,
it's a very boring day,
there is nothing much to look at,
there is nothing much to say,"

The kids all nodded. They knew what
that felt like.

"But then," Mr. Prelutsky went on, "a
poem might take an unexpected turn.

"there's a peacock on my sneakers,
there's a penguin on my head,
there's a dormouse on my doorstep,
I am going back to bed."

Fern smiled. She pictured what she'd

look like with a peacock on her sneakers and a penguin on her head.

"Today is very boring,
it is boring through and through,
there is absolutely nothing
that I think I want to do,
I see giants riding rhinos,
and an ogre with a sword,
there's a dragon blowing smoke rings,
I am positively bored."

Suddenly, Buster saw Binky chasing him with a sword while a dragon swooped down breathing fire. Luckily, Buster ducked at the last second — and the dragon crashed into Binky, leaving them both a bit dazed.

Mr. Prelutsky stifled a yawn. Then he continued.

"Today is very boring,
I can hardly help but yawn,
there's a flying saucer landing
in the middle of my lawn,"

Muffy saw herself all dressed up, stepping forward to greet the visiting aliens. Such travelers would have shopped in some very unusual places. She would love to know what they found there.

"A volcano just erupted
less than half a mile away,
and I think I felt an earthquake,
it's a very boring day."

Binky imagined a volcano erupting, the lava pouring down the sides. While people screamed and ran for their lives, Binky watched as the lava engulfed Lakewood Elementary School.

"No homework tonight," he said with a sigh.

"Pay attention!" whispered Fern, prompting him to clap along with the other kids.

"Thank you, thank you," said Mr. Prelutsky. "But now I want to hear from you. Let's have our first contestant."

Nobody said anything. They were all too nervous.

"Come now," said Mr. Prelutsky, "we're all friends here. All right, then — I'll pick someone. Let's see. . . ." He consulted his list. "Well, the first one of you to sign up might have some enthusiam for poetry. Where are you, Fern?"

There was no chance to escape, especially when everyone turned to stare at her.

"Here," she said meekly — looking a little pale.

Chapter 8

Fern stood up. Although she loved writing poetry, she hadn't thought about actually reciting her poem. It was a strange feeling. She started out slowly. Her poem was about the fall and the change of seasons. It was sad in a way, but it was also hopeful, for as a season passes, it brings hope of a new season to follow.

Everyone was quiet as Fern's soft voice reached out into the room. When she saw how attentive everyone had become, her confidence grew. Her voice strengthened as she came toward the end.

"And the ghosts of fallen trees weep,
For a world that can't live without them."

Fern was done. There was silence for a moment. Then Mr. Prelutsky led the applause.

"Excellent!" he declared. "And beautifully read."

"Thank you," said Fern. "That means a lot to me, because I have all of your books."

"Really?" Mr. Prelutsky looked pleased. "You are obviously a girl with impeccable taste. So who's next? Any volunteers? No?" He consulted his list. "Ah, yes . . . Francine Frensky."

"That's me!" said Francine, bolting up.

"There's a notation here. . . ." said Mr. Prelutsky. "I see that you also have a musical accompaniment and visual aids. Wonderful! And your piece, I believe, is entitled 'Hockey Puck Headache.' "

"That's right."

Francine walked up to the front of the room carrying a bunch of pictures. She nodded to Muffy, who began playing a steady beat on a set of bongo drums. As Francine read each line, she held up a picture illustrating it.

"My dad took me to a hockey game,
I got hit in the head by a puck.
I yelled out — Ow! My head! Ow!
Call an ambulance! Ouch! Ow!
Oh, brother — this hurts!
Put ice on it,
It's gonna swell!
I got a big old purple lump on my head,
And used it for show-and-tell."

The picture of Francine with a big lump on her head got the loudest laugh. When she finished, she made a little bow. The audience cheered.

"Performance art!" said Mr. Prelutsky. "Very inventive. I love it."

"I'll go next!" Binky shouted.

He stood up.

"People think I can't write a poem.
But they're so wrong.
I can write a poem.
I wrote this one.
I wrote this poem,
And I gave it the title 'Binky's Poem,'
So shut up. The end."

The applause was a little slow in coming, but it picked up after Binky glared at everyone.

"That's not a poem," Muffy whispered to Francine. "He rhymed *poem* with *poem* — three times."

"Are you going to remind him of that?" said Francine.

Muffy decided against it.

The poems continued, but Fern kept looking around. Someone was missing, someone who had promised to be there. Finally, she turned to Buster. "Where's Arthur?" she whispered.

Chapter 9

• • • • • • • • • • •

"THEY CAUGHT THE GORILLA!"

"I heard, D.W.," said Arthur. "It was on the radio." He didn't look up from the paper he was writing on.

"Joey was in the woods all night. I'll bet he was cold and lonely. He should have come to our house. Don't you think he would have been happier here, Arthur?"

The only sound in the room was Arthur's pen scribbling on the paper.

"Arthur?"

"Whatever you say, D.W. There! I'm finished. I'm late for the poetry contest. See you —"

He rushed out the door.

At the library, Buster had begun to read.

"When a dirty sock
Drops on your face, P.U.
When your friend's baby sister
Starts to spew.
Half a worm in the apple you bit."

The Brain began to turn a little green, and he grabbed ahold of his stomach.

"Finding a human bone in your Jell-O.
Blowing nose-slime green and yellow."

Francine sank under the table. She looked very sorry she had eaten such a big lunch.

"And people who eat creamed corn
With their mouths open

So you can see it."

Buster then made a little bow. Apparently, he was finished.

Binky applauded wildly. Everyone else looked sick.

Mr. Prelutsky took a deep breath. "Well, that was very, uh, vivid, Buster. I probably shouldn't mention the free tapioca pudding that will be served at the reception."

Everyone groaned.

Ms. Turner stepped forward. "Now, our special guest will choose the winning poem."

The door flew open and Arthur burst in.

"Am I too late? I couldn't get past the crosswalk. First, there were little kids, then a circus parade. And you know those elephants, they like to take their time."

He ran up to Mr. Prelutsky and whispered in his ear.

The famous poet nodded. "All right,

then," he said, "our final, final, FINAL poem is 'Joey Goes to the City' by Arthur Read."

Arthur took out his poem and began reading.

"Joey was a happy ape
Until some hunters caught him,
He liked the jungle better than
The city where they brought him."

Arthur could imagine Joey was happily playing with a paddleball and string — until a cage suddenly dropped on top of him. He was placed on a large truck and taken from the jungle into the city.

"The city was louder,
The city was meaner,
Even the dirt
In the jungle was cleaner.

"So Joey decided to
Make a daring escape,
The hunters were suddenly
Minus one ape."

Joey bent the bars of his cage and hopped out. As people fled before him, he climbed to the top of a building to look for the jungle.

"He climbed the tallest building
Because from there he'd see
How far away the jungle was
From the middle of the city.

"Joey jumped into
A passing plane
But the pilot didn't wait
For him to explain."

Joey consulted the flying manual while he steered with his feet. He finally made it back home.

"Joey flew back to the jungle
And told his ape friends in their lair,
'The city's okay for a visit,
But you wouldn't want to live there.' "

Chapter 10

• • • • • • • • • • •

The kids all applauded. Arthur smiled.

"A poem grown from today's head-lines," said Mr. Prelutsky. "Topical, yet timeless. Very good, very good. And now we wait for the judges to announce the winner of the contest. In this case, of course, I'm the only judge. So my decision will be final. Drum roll, please."

He pointed to Muffy, who began beating her bongos furiously.

Boom-ba-da. Boom-ba-da. Boom-ba-da-boom.

Mr. Prelutsky paused. "You know what? I hate singling out one winner when everyone did such a terrific job. In my opinion, you all win!"

The audience cheered.

"And now for the pudding," said Ms. Turner, leading Mr. Prelutsky to the refreshment table.

Fern sighed. "You all won the bet. So nobody has to join the Poetry Club."

The kids gathered around her.

"But this was fun!" said Arthur.

"Yeah!" Buster agreed. "And I know lots of other disgusting stuff. I've barely scratched the surface."

"I want to play more bongos," said Muffy.

Binky pushed the others aside and marched right up to Fern.

"You know what I have to say to you?"

"What?" Fern said meekly.

"That we don't have to do what you say. You can't stop us if we want to join."

"Hey!" said Francine. "The sign-up list

is over here."

The kids crowded around to sign up.

Fern walked over to shake Mr. Prelutsky's hand.

"I was wondering...," Fern began.

"Yes?" said Mr. Prelutsky.

"Could you maybe recite another poem?"

All the other kids shouted out in agreement.

"All right," said Mr. Prelutsky. "Well, Buster's poem reminded me of one of my own. It's called 'Jellyfish Stew.' "

As his voice filled the room, visions of jellyfish stew swam through everyone's thoughts. When it was time to eat the tapioca pudding, nobody seemed very hungry.

Good poetry, after all, can be very filling.